Gruesome and Bloodsocks

'I warned you, Augusta,' said Uncle Batticoop, 'but you took no heed. All I have to say now is that you're a disgrace to the whole vampire kingdom. You'll have to go. You'll make us a laughing stock.'

Gruesome stared sullenly at the ground. It wasn't her fault. She couldn't help it if blood made her sick and brought her out in silver spots. 'OK,' she said. 'I'm leaving, and good riddance to you.' Gruesome felt a rush of air overhead as five dark bat-shapes passed. She turned in the other direction.

Also available in Young Lions

Simon and the Witch *Margaret Stuart Barry*
The Julian Stories *Ann Cameron*
The Lily Pickle Band Book *Gwen Grant*
Gruesome and Bloodsocks Move House *Jane Holiday*
Gruesome and Bloodsocks on Wheels *Jane Holiday*
Floella Hits the Roof *Jane Holiday*
Bunnicula *James and Deborah Howe*
Lucy and the Big Bad Wolf *Ann Jungman*
Hairy Tales and Nursery Crimes *Michael Rosen*

Gruesome and Bloodsocks

JANE HOLIDAY

Illustrated by Steven Appleby

Young Lions

First published in Great Britain by Granada Publishing in 1984
Published by Dragon Books in 1985
First published in Young Lions in 1989

Young Lions is an imprint of
the Children's Division, part of
the Collins Publishing Group,
8 Grafton Street, London W1X 3LA

Printed and bound in Great Britain by
William Collins Sons & Co. Ltd, Glasgow

1

'This is your last chance Augusta,' said Uncle Batticoop grimly. 'Your very last chance.'

The other vampires – Annelid, Hirudinea, Hideous Hattie and Five-fanged Francis all stared menacingly at Augusta (otherwise known as Gruesome Gussie). It was after midnight and they were eager to set out on their nightly blood-hunting expedition. Gruesome, though, found it hard to stop yawning. She preferred to sleep on a nice damp tombstone at night but the others would never leave her alone.

'You have never,' said Uncle Batticoop, flicking a dead moth off his dingy top hat, 'since taking up your residence in this churchyard, been known to let any blood pass your lips.' (He was given the title 'Uncle' because he was the leader of the group. He was at least a hundred years older than anyone else.)

'Disgusting,' murmured Hideous Hattie, while the others hissed and tutted, and looked at poor Gruesome with loathing.

'We've taken you with us many, many times,' said Uncle Batticoop.

'Innumerable times,' said Five-fanged Francis, displaying to the full his three extra fangs (the envy of every vampire for miles around).

'But never,' said Uncle Batticoop, 'NEVER have you made the slightest effort to obtain any blood for yourself.'

A chorus of tuttings and hissings broke out once more among the assembled vampires.

'When Hideous Hattie (out of the blood of human kindness) tried to feed you some from a spoon,' he continued, frowning at Five-fanged Francis, who was dancing up and down with excitement, 'what happened? You *spat* it out.'

'Spat out best blood,' said Hideous Hattie, wailing afresh at the horror of the recollection.

'And then you were sick,' continued Uncle Batticoop.

'I couldn't help it,' said Gruesome. 'And I couldn't help it if it brought me out in spots either.'

'SILVER spots,' said Five-fanged Francis as if this made it all very much worse.

'I don't like the taste of blood,' said Gruesome. 'I can't help it. I'll drink Coca Cola – that's just the same colour.' (She had once found a half-empty can on a rubbish tip not far from the churchyard and had drunk the contents eagerly. Since then she had always looked out for other cans.)

'Coca Cola,' sneered Uncle Batticoop. 'Who ever heard of a vampire living on Coca Cola? No, Augusta. Tonight is your last chance. Your very last

chance. Well, hurry up then,' he said impatiently, as Gruesome just stood there. 'METAMORPHOSE, Augusta. CHANGE YOUR SHAPE.' The others had of course already metamorphosed into their nightly bat-shapes without needing to be told.

Now the six of them each gave a backwards leap into flight and were soon swooping over the fields next to the churchyard.

Uncle Batticoop soon spotted a likely prey – a cow left out over night.

'That will do very nicely,' he said, as they descended in a neat V-formation. They landed swiftly and silently by the sleeping cow.

'Excellent,' whispered Uncle Batticoop, bristling with satisfaction. 'You may well find beef blood more palatable, Augusta. I know a lot of vampires prefer it. Some human blood is very low grade, I must admit.'

He positioned them round the animal so that Annelid and Hirudinea were at the ear, Hideous Hattie and Five-fanged Francis were at the thin skin round the tail, and he and Gruesome were at the neck.

While the others started to lap, Uncle Batticoop once more explained to Gruesome the correct procedure.

'Just a quick nip with your fangs to open a divot of skin like this,' he said. 'Then cover the place with your saliva – so! That stops the blood clotting.' He could restrain himself no longer and began greedily lapping the blood into his mouth through the groove in his lower lip. As soon as Gruesome saw they were busy, she leapt backwards into flight and was off.

'I'll be sick if I stay a moment longer,' she thought. 'I don't even like the *smell* of it.'

She knew it would take them about a quarter of an hour to drink their fill. Then, bloated, they would make their way home to the churchyard and would spend the remaining hours till dawn dancing over the tombstones and chanting eerily.

Some nights they spent all the dark hours searching fruitlessly for prey and would return miserably just before dawn to creep into all the most unsavoury cracks and crevices and holes they could find.

All except Gruesome, that is. How she loved the daylight when the others were dead to the world and she and Bloodsocks (her cat) could relax on the tombstones.

Gruesome flew round for some time, finally sinking down on the vicarage roof. She dared not go back to the churchyard till daylight when they would all be asleep. Uncle Batticoop would be so angry with her.

She sighed as she wondered for the trillionth time why they couldn't just leave her alone. She would drink anything else she could find and she ate most things as well; although in the churchyard she could find only twigs, tree bark and insects. Bloodsocks enjoyed fieldmice, voles and the occasional unwary bird which did not expect to find cats in a churchyard. He never came on any blood-hunting expeditions, when she was dragged out by the others. He preferred to curl up cosily under a tree until her return.

From the safety of the vicarage roof, Gruesome saw the five bloated bat-shapes return and land in the churchyard. She shivered as she thought of Uncle

Batticoop's rage and the vicious nips and bites they would give her if she were there (particularly Five-fanged Francis).

'It's for your own good, Augusta,' Uncle Batticoop would say, whenever Gruesome said it wasn't fair. 'You *must* learn the correct rules of behaviour.'

At last it was daylight and she could safely return to the churchyard. She flew down, first of all seeking out Bloodsocks, who was stretched beneath a yew tree. The two of them sat down together on her favourite tombstone in the corner, overgrown with moss and with a discoloured stone angel at its head.

'I wonder what he meant by my "last chance", Bloodsocks,' she said. 'What do you think he's going to do?'

2

She found out soon enough when, at midnight, she was awoken by a vicious bite. It was Five-fanged Francis.

'Ouch!' cried Gruesome. 'You ought to get your talons trimmed.'

'What happened to you last night?' he hissed. 'You flew off without telling anyone.'

'None of you would have noticed anyway,' said Gruesome. 'You were all stuffing yourselves as if blood were going out of fashion. Ouch! Leave me alone. Go away!'

'Augusta,' bellowed Uncle Batticoop. 'Come here!'

Five-fanged Francis sniggered as he slunk off. 'You've had it this time, Augusta – you and that stupid cat of yours.'

Uncle Batticoop called again. Gruesome knew that voice. It meant his special meeting to discuss something important. She ran.

The sky was dark and starless. Light rain beat on the tombstones. All five of them were lined up, barely visible in the darkness, when she arrived with Bloodsocks close at her heels. The two of them huddled together by the yew tree.

Hardly a sound was to be heard save the distant hooting of an owl. Bloodsocks tensed, his claws digging into Gruesome's shoulder. Uncle Batticoop and the other four stared at them for some time in silence.

'I warned you, Augusta,' he said at last, 'but you took no heed. I warned you that it was your last chance. All I have to say now' (I wish it was all he had to say, thought Gruesome, who knew he would go on for ages) 'is BEGONE. Never darken this churchyard again. Begone, Augusta!'

'Begone, Augusta,' echoed Annelid, Hirudinea, Hideous Hattie and Five-fanged Francis.

'Begone,' they all hissed yet again.

'Why?' asked Gruesome. 'It's not fair. You can't just drive me away like this.'

'You know very well why,' said Uncle Batticoop. 'You're a disgrace to the whole vampire kingdom. You seem to forget that we're descended from a long line of Transylvanian vampires. Your conduct has always been unsatisfactory . . .'

'Always,' repeated Annelid, Hirudinea and Hideous Hattie.

'Unsatisfactory,' said Five-fanged Francis.

Gruesome glared at him, forgetting her fear. She wouldn't miss *him* anyway, big-headed prig – or did she mean big-fanged prig? She smiled to herself.

'There you are,' hissed Uncle Batticoop. 'Just what I mean. NOT listening.'

All the other vampires (apart from Gruesome) howled sympathetically.

'First of all,' said Uncle Batticoop, 'you're always WALKING about in the DAYTIME, when any self-respecting vampire would be tucked up fast asleep in his coffin.'

'HER coffin,' Gruesome muttered to herself.

11

'Talking through her fangs again,' announced Five-fanged Francis with satisfaction.

'Second of all,' said Uncle Batticoop, giving Five-fanged Francis a tap on the head with a funeral urn, 'at the very time when you should be WIDE AWAKE and thirsting for adventure (not to mention blood) . . .'

'Wide awake,' sneered Hideous Hattie. 'Augusta? That'll be the day.'

Uncle Batticoop was beginning to grind his fangs in rage at being interrupted so many times.

'As I said,' he continued loudly, 'when you should be wide awake and searching for a nice throatful of blood' (here they all stared at poor Gruesome who was, of course, yawning) 'YOU,' Uncle Batticoop dropped his voice, 'go to sleep or sneak off when no one's looking – as you did last night.'

All five vampires shook their heads and stared horribly at Gruesome.

'Third of all, and by far the worst,' he continued, 'you are ALLERGIC to blood.'

Gruesome stared sullenly at the ground. It wasn't her fault. She couldn't help it if blood made her sick and brought her out in silver spots. They had tried all kinds of blood on her, from bats' blood to human (including, of course, last night's cow blood), but to no avail. The smell made her sick.

They boiled it.

She still didn't like it.

They chilled it.

That was even worse.

They tried mixing the blood with everything from shredded hemlock to powdered mouse droppings.

13

Nothing, however, made the slightest difference. She just couldn't keep it down.

'All you ever drink is Coca Cola,' said Uncle Batticoop. 'Coca Cola! What a disgrace.'

'Not a proper vampire! Not a proper vampire!' chanted Five-fanged Francis.

Gruesome said nothing. What was there to say? She couldn't change the way she was made. She was a misfit.

'You'll have to go,' said Uncle Batticoop. 'You'll make us all a laughing stock.'

The rest howled in agreement.

'OK. I'm leaving and good riddance to you,' Gruesome said (for none of them had ever been kind to her). 'Come on, Bloodsocks.'

Bloodsocks leapt off her shoulder and together they left the churchyard. As she made her way out into the road, Gruesome felt a rush of air overhead as five dark bat-shapes passed. It was Uncle Batticoop, Annelid, Hirudinea, Hideous Hattie and Five-fanged Francis flying towards the town in search of prey. Gruesome turned in the other direction – towards Trumpington. She sought fresh fields and churchyards new.

3

It was early summer, two weeks since Gruesome had left Lower Barton. She lay flat on her back in Trumpington churchyard with Bloodsocks curled up on her feet spitting out mousebones. The sun shone and huge white clouds pillowed out in the sky. All at once the peace of the afternoon was shattered.

'Hey! Hey you!'

Gruesome continued to look up at the sky.

'Hey you,' came the voice again.

She looked round to see a tubby man in a green boilersuit and wellington boots stomping towards her. (It was Big Pete, Trumpington's gravedigger.)

'Here, you shouldn't be lying on a grave. That's wrong, that is. What are you doing here anyway?'

Gruesome sat up and brushed her long black hair off her pale green face. Her dress, also long and black, was crumpled and stained with moss.

'I've moved in here,' she said. 'This is my home.'

'Eh?' said Big Pete. 'Don't be daft. No one lives here.' He laughed loudly. 'You must have come while I was on my holidays last week. Get off that grave, will you! It's not decent.'

He pointed to a large tree-stump. 'That's where I usually eat my butties. Sit there if you like.'

They sat down together on the tree-stump. 'It's my tea-break,' said Big Pete. 'Want some pork pie? You look a bit hungry to me.'

Gruesome chewed the pie carefully and found to her surprise that she liked it. She liked, too, the mug of tea Big Pete gave her 'to swill it down, like'. It was much better than blood. Gruesome told him what had happened and why she had moved to Trumpington.

'Vampire, eh?' said Big Pete. 'No wonder your face is green. No decent food, I shouldn't wonder. Here, you'd better have this other piece of pie. I was saving it, like, but I reckon you could do with it.'

Gruesome took it with pleasure and crumbled a bit up for Bloodsocks.

'I've never come across no vampires here before and I've been a gravedigger here now, man and boy, for twenty years. Sure as my name's Pete Hardisty.'

'My name's Augusta – Gussie for short – but all my friends call me Gruesome.'

'All what friends? Don't look to me as if you've got any.'

16

It was true, thought Gruesome. She didn't know anyone except Annelid, Hirudinea, Hideous Hattie, Five-fanged Francis and Uncle Batticoop.

'Well, there's Bloodsocks,' she said, pointing to him. 'He's my friend.'

'Bloodsocks? That's a rum name for a cat.'

'No it isn't,' said Gruesome. 'He's black all over except for the ends of his paws. And they're rusty-brown, just the colour of dried blood.'

'Never mind that,' said Big Pete. 'You can't stay here, vampire or not. The council won't allow it.'

'But I've nowhere else to go,' wailed Gruesome. 'I've just found a nice cosy tombstone for the two of us, and now you say we must go. Bloodsocks hasn't even had time to lay in a good store of fieldmice yet.'

'Don't worry about it,' said Big Pete. 'I dare say the council will find you a house. We don't have any homeless – not in Trumpington. I'll tell Arthur from the Housing to drop by. He'll know what to do. I'll be off now. Have to trim the vicar's front hedge. Ta ta . . . er . . . Gussie.'

'Call me Gruesome,' she called after him as he marched off.

4

Gruesome certainly didn't want to live in a house, but the council would not allow her to stay in Trumpington churchyard. She might spend months going from churchyard to churchyard and being turned away, so at last she had to give in. In due course she was allocated a council flat and told to report to the DHSS.

'You don't need to worry about the rent, love,' said the man from the council. 'We pay your rent till you find yourself a job. But you'll need summat to live on.' He gave Gruesome a sheaf of forms and a reply-paid envelope and told her how to sign on.

Eventually Gruesome found the vast four-storied building opposite the Public Library. She went in and out of several doors and up and down flights of stairs. At last someone told her she needed 'Fresh Claims'.

'Go round the back,' she was told, 'and in at the side door.'

Inside, there were five separate queues of people waiting behind different numbers along the counter. On the left hand side was a muddle of people, some sitting on hard red chairs bolted to the ground, others grouped untidily round the counter. ENQUIRIES said a notice above it.

Two children were playing noughts-and-crosses on the floor with sticks of chalk. A baby in a push-chair was crying. All the time people of all shapes, sizes and ages pushed in and out of the swing doors at either end of the huge room.

No one took any notice of Gruesome. They were all intent on their own business and didn't want to lose their places in their particular queues.

She stood at the back, leaning against a cream-painted radiator. On the notice-board to the left of her were pinned numerous leaflets. Gruesome was glad she had spent time teaching herself to read from the faded epitaphs carved on tombstones. It looked as if it might come in useful. She had even learned to write by copying the letters, using earth-worms. The trouble was that sometimes a worm would crawl away in the middle of a word or change itself from a letter S to an O or a C instead of quietly staying put. Or Bloodsocks would come along and eat one of them before she could stop him. (Bloodsocks was very partial to raw earth-worm.)

At last it was Gruesome's turn to approach the counter. She handed over the note the man from the council had given her.

The clerk behind the counter was wearing a pink T-shirt and jeans. She had lots of hair which stuck out in frizzed ringlets all round her face. Little gold stars hung from her ears and three pink bangles adorned her left arm. She read the note, looked once at Gruesome's fangs and then looked some-where just above her head as she spoke to her.

'Mm . . . so you're moving into 52A Wellington Street . . . And you have no job at present . . . What was your previous address?'

'Er . . . I lived with some other . . . er . . . some others,' said Gruesome, 'in a churchyard.'

The clerk momentarily transferred her gaze to Gruesome's face and then looked back to the spot above her head again.

'I see. Sleeping rough.' She sniffed. 'So you've not been working? What was the last paid job you had?'

Gruesome had to confess she'd never had one, also that she had no O levels or CSEs, didn't know her age, had no insurance card and had never been to school.

'But you MUST have,' the clerk said. 'Everybody goes to school.'

'I . . . I moved about a lot,' said Gruesome, trying to be helpful.

'I see,' said the girl, sniffing again. 'No job experience, no qualifications, no insurance card. I don't suppose you've got a birth certificate.'

She wrote several sentences on a notepad. 'This is very irregular, Miss . . . er . . . Miss Vampire,' she said quickly, looking even higher in the air above Gruesome than before, so that Gruesome turned round to see what she was looking at. 'We've never had anybody without records before. You'll have to find out how old you are – or it could cause difficulties when it's time for your retirement.'

Gruesome looked blank.

'Your old age pension,' explained the clerk, speaking very slowly. 'You get it when you're sixty. Still, that's not our worry at the moment. Now, you're not entitled to any unemployment benefit so you'll have to fill in a BI form and take it to the Supplementary Benefit office. I'll fill it in for you, if

you like.' She put the form in a brown envelope and gave it to Gruesome with several leaflets and a white card.

'This is your UB40 – your signing-on card. You must come here every other Monday at 9.45, starting next Monday. OK?'

Gruesome nodded.

'If you get a job, just post this card back to us. Now, you must take this envelope to the office round the corner. It's the second door down. Turn left when you go in the main door. It's room 101. Goodbye – next, please.'

Gruesome trudged off.

The next room she entered was also stuffed with people, some sitting on red chairs bolted to the floor, others leaning against the sludge green walls. A large NO SMOKING sign covered with burn marks hung on the far wall. The air was thick with smoke. An oldish man was asleep, stretched over four chairs with his head on his rolled-up jacket. Two children were juggling tennis-balls. Another, older girl was gouging a message to the Prime Minister on one wall with a penknife. She turned and stared at Gruesome for a couple of seconds and then resumed her occupation.

It was late by the time Gruesome at last left the building. She'd had to answer the same questions all over again as well as a lot more besides. The clerk then read out all the answers she had given and made her sign it at the bottom. Gruesome was just able to manage 'A Vampire', though she had never written with a pen before. It was better than worms, she thought.

'Of course, while you're unemployed, you're entitled to free spectacles if required, and . . . er . . . free dental treatment,' he said.

He also seemed to be looking at something just above her head, thought Gruesome.

'You'll receive your giro as soon as your claim has been processed.'

· At last, Gruesome could go to her new abode. First of all, though, she had to collect Bloodsocks whom she had left at the churchyard. She had asked Big Pete to keep an eye on him.

She found Bloodsocks a bit peevish because she had been so long.

'I reckon you're the first vampire in history to rent a council flat,' said Big Pete, '*and* to sign on the dole.'

Gruesome departed sadly with Bloodsocks. How would she ever be able to live in a house, she wondered. She felt ill after sitting in those big rooms all day. And she was sure Bloodsocks wouldn't like it either.

5

Big Pete insisted on bringing Gruesome a van-load of second-hand furniture 'to make it more homely, like'. Gruesome didn't really care if there was any furniture or not. When her giro came at last, however, and she had cashed it at the post office at the end of Enfield Street, she did buy herself a good strong coffin on HP from the undertaker's. Mr Jackson (the undertaker) was a bit doubtful about the proceedings at first.

'It's not the way people usually do things,' he explained. 'Sometimes they take out an account and save some money with us for their funeral, but they don't usually want the coffin beforehand.

He looked at Gruesome's pale green face and bony green hands and her bare feet protruding from under the ancient black dress. 'They're quite costly. Unfortunately,' he coughed, 'a coffin's not something that can be bought second-hand.'

At last Gruesome, using Big Pete Hardisty as a reference, persuaded him to let her have one on HP.

'We'll deliver it by van,' he said, 'not our usual cars. It might worry the neighbours.'

Once the coffin had arrived and Gruesome had installed it in her bedroom, she felt a bit better. She hung dried viperskins on the walls and black plastic bin-liners at the windows.

She and Bloodsocks shared the house with

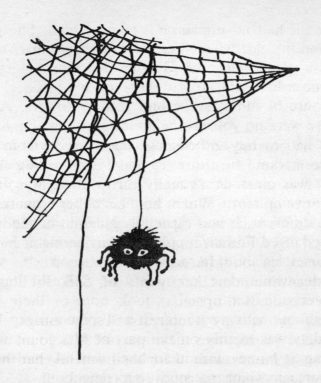

Hairietta and Marcus. Hairietta was a spider who climbed in through the kitchen window one day. She spun a huge web which stretched from one corner of the ceiling right across to the cooker. Marcus was a frog Gruesome found lurking behind a dustbin in the Royal Arcade. She brought him home and he had taken up residence in the bath.

The flat was the bottom half of an end-terrace house. At the back of the house was a small yard where rosebay willowherb pushed up through the flags and grew up the drainpipe.

Gruesome felt very strange in Trumpington. The pavements felt harsh and cold to her bare feet and she had to buy herself a pair of cheap canvas shoes.

The air had an unpleasant, smoky smell. She preferred the earthy smell of the churchyard after rain. Most of all she missed the delicious fragrance (almost like a taste, to her) of tombstones – a mixture of moss, stone and rotting flowers. Also, there were no voles or fieldmice scuttling about and she had to buy Bloodsocks tins of food from the supermarket.

It was pleasant, though, not to have any of the other vampires around to grumble at her because she was different. It was especially pleasant not to have Five-fanged Francis nipping her or jeering at her or telling tales about her to Uncle Batticoop.

Meanwhile, the occupants of 52B Wellington Street (the flat upstairs) took note of their new neighbour with great interest and some anxiety. The anxiety was mainly on the part of Mrs Jones who, being at home more than her husband, had more leisure in which to study her neighbour at close quarters.

Mr Jones was one of the few in Wellington Street to be in employment. He was a plumber and, apart from working for 'Trumpington Plastics', did a few 'foreigners' from time to time as occasion arose.

Leotard, their son, was at first disappointed when he found no children were moving in below. Grown-ups were all much of a muchness, he reckoned, not interested in anything except making you uncomfortable in some way, whether it was at home or at school. He could see, though, that their new neighbour was a bit different from the normal run of grown-ups. She obviously didn't care what she looked like, and she didn't go mad cleaning windows and scrubbing doorsteps or similar daft things, like most of them in Wellington Street. Old Mrs Thomas, for instance, scrubbed hers twice a day.

'You could eat off her doorstep,' his mother said once. What was the point, wondered Leotard. People didn't want to eat off doorsteps.

Mrs Jones was a small, wiry woman with dyed blonde hair. She had a grown-up married daughter of twenty-two, so Leotard was like an only child. She worked part-time in the newsagent's at Trumpington railway station and Leotard was very often left to his own devices.

'I suppose I ought to pop down and have a word with her, Dave,' Mrs Jones said to her husband as they sat over their evening meal of pork chops, oven chips and peas, 'though she looked a bit odd to me. Leotard, get the Arctic Roll out of the fridge and put the kettle on for some tea, there's a love.'

'Why not?' said her husband. 'Best to be on good terms, seeing she's underneath us. Just her, is there?'

So it was that next morning Gruesome found Mrs Jones, wearing a pale green crimplene dress and brown wedge sandals, at her door.

'Hallo. I'm Jean Jones from upstairs. I just thought . . .' Mrs Jones faltered for a moment as she took in Gruesome's appearance and felt something furry brush against her legs.

Gruesome smiled; at which Mrs Jones backed away. She bumped clumsily into Bloodsocks, who spat and fled.

'I'm Augusta, otherwise known as Gruesome. Come in.'

'Well . . . er . . . ,' said Mrs Jones, peering in over

27

Gruesome's shoulder and noting the viperskins, the dustbin liners, the uncarpeted floor and the cobwebs. 'I can see you haven't unpacked properly yet. I'll look in when you're more settled. Goodbye for now. Goodbye.'

Gruesome was disappointed. 'I wonder why she said that, Bloodie,' she pondered as she went back inside. 'I *am* settled in. I wonder what *her* house is like.'

Bloodsocks purred as he watched Gruesome puncture a tin of 'Katkins' with a fang. It was good to be fed out of a tin. Much less trouble, he thought.

6

'You never saw anything like it,' Mrs Jones repeated that night. 'Full of cobwebs and dust, and she's got bin-liners tacked across the windows just like the black-out in the old days. She must be mad.'

'How old is she?' asked her husband, momentarily distracted from the sports news. 'Perhaps she remembers the last war. Maybe she was in an air-raid and is still a bit confused.'

'Like Gran,' said Leotard, scratching one ear and adjusting the set of his cap.

'Your Gran is not confused,' said his mother fiercely, completely diverted from the question of her neighbour's age.

'No,' said Leotard. 'I mean she remembers the war. She was telling me all about air-raids and black-outs and stuff. D'you reckon Thingy downstairs got bombed or something and went off her nut? Perhaps she'll run amok in the street.'

'Don't be daft,' said his dad. 'Here, take that cap off in the house. Frightened your head'll get cold or something?' He guffawed loudly, stopping abruptly when Leotard took off his cap to reveal a completely bald head.

'Here, what you done that for? Eh, Jean, what's he shaved all his hair off for?'

His wife shrugged her shoulders. 'He would have

it. He got our Ron to do it for him in the end. Thought it was right funny, he did.'

'He would,' said Mr Jones, looking morose at the mention of his son-in-law. 'Great lummocks! Good job it's the holidays, eh lad? Dunno what the teacher'd say.'

'Daft,' said his mother. 'Still, it's him that'll have to put up with all the comments. I'm not bothered if he wants to go round looking like a cross between a mugger and one of them Hairy Krishnas. That's his lookout.'

'I like it,' said Leotard, twiddling his earring.

'Good job,' said his father. ''Cause it'll take the heck of a long time to grow back. Makes your ears look like jug handles.'

'You should see her downstairs,' said his wife. 'She's really odd-looking.'

'Why? What's she like?' Leotard asked. He hadn't seen her close to. He rushed to the window to look down into the back yard.

'Never you mind,' said his mother. 'You're to keep well away, you hear. I don't want you having nothing to do with her.'

Meanwhile, Gruesome was gradually getting to know the other people in the street. She had invested in some new, colourful dresses which, although they too reached her ankles and made her look eccentric in a place like Trumpington, did make her a slightly less sinister figure. She'd also bought a pair of black plimsolls to alternate with the heavy canvas shoes. She had noticed that people in the street had several different outfits of clothes which they wore on different days of the week.

She said 'Hello' to old Mrs Thomas one morning as she was cleaning her front doorstep. Mrs Thomas lived all alone except for Susie, her Scottie dog, and loved to have someone to talk to. She was quite old and couldn't see very well, even with spectacles, so she didn't notice anything especially odd about Gruesome.

Before much longer, Gruesome knew all about Mrs Thomas's long-dead husband, her children and grandchildren in Canada, how expensive it was feeding Susie, and the best way to clean doorsteps.

She also got to know the Patel twins (both boys) who lived in the corner shop and sometimes served behind the counter. They didn't stare at her oddly either, but even showed her the pet rabbit they kept in their back yard.

A side road, Enfield Street, ran up past Gruesome's flat. Opposite 52A and B, on the other side of this street, lived Mr Todd. He had a butcher's shop a couple of miles or so away in the middle of Trumpington. Gruesome had seen his van outside the house. She was glad his shop was not actually in Wellington Street where she might have been able to smell the blood.

Although Gruesome gradually found her way about, she didn't like being shut up inside four walls. Without a roof it might be better, she thought, so she could stare right up to the stars at night. Because it felt so airless she left all the doors and windows open, day and night. One morning, however, she received a visit from a policeman.

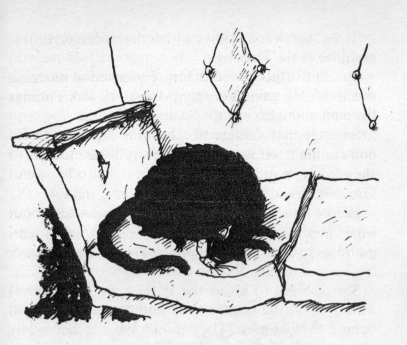

'Come in,' said Gruesome.

The policeman took his helmet off and sat down on the battered old settee which Big Pete had brought round. 'Booooooooiiiiiiiinnnnnnngggggggg' it went, as it always did when it was sat upon. The policeman looked round, rather dubiously, at the furnishings.

'Would you like a glass of cabbage juice?' Gruesome asked. (She'd found out that people usually offered visitors a drink from careful watching of the old black-and-white television set, also brought by Big Pete.)

'No thanks, love,' said the policeman. 'Not while I'm driving.'

Then he gave her a long lecture about shutting all doors and windows at night.

'It's a wonder you haven't been murdered in your bed,' he said. 'That Mrs Jones upstairs told me you were a bit forgetful, like. Quite worried about you, she was.' He gave Bloodsocks a quick tickle under the chin and left.

So after that Gruesome shut her doors and windows at night. 'If it gets really stuffy,' she thought, 'I can always sleep in the garden.'

It felt dreadful at first. Gruesome thought she wouldn't be able to breathe. She almost wished she were back in Lower Barton churchyard again with the others. Then she thought of Five-fanged Francis

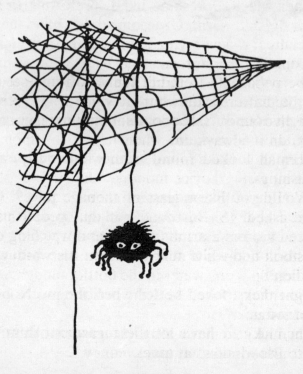

and the way he would sneak up and nip her just when she was falling asleep, and Uncle Batticoop's lectures. Anything was better than that, she decided. Besides, she wasn't alone. She had Hairietta, whose web had now vastly increased and contained large numbers of flies of various species waiting to be devoured. And there was Marcus, too. She had found him a companion now and had stocked the bath with some suitable plant-life for the two of them. Best of all, there was Bloodsocks, her friend and lifelong companion.

Bloodsocks didn't seem to mind being shut in, Gruesome noticed, as long as they were together. Indeed, he had always disliked the wet and stormy weather which Gruesome liked, preferring to keep his fur dry and warm. Gruesome didn't mind the sun, especially if she was lying in the open air, preferably on a tombstone; but rain and wind seemed to her more natural. She couldn't see why people took to their heels at once when it rained, or bundled themselves up into shiny coats, boots and hats so that it wouldn't touch them.

'They sit in baths full of water without any clothes on at all when they're indoors,' she said to Bloodsocks. 'I just don't understand them.'

Occasionally Gruesome picked some thistles, white nettle flowers and dandelions out of the garden and stood them in a milk bottle on the window-sill. She didn't put any water in the bottle, though, as she thought they looked better when they were brown and dried-up.

'I'm lucky to have all these garden plants,' she said to Bloodsocks. 'It saves money.'

She became adept at making egg and nettle loaf, dandelion tea-cakes and fish and thistle trifle.

But it wasn't long though before Gruesome found living in Trumpington had its disadvantages.

7

The main trouble was Bloodsocks. He chased the ducks in Trumpington Park, and frightened one of them so much that it went into hiding for a week.

'If I ever see that cat round here again,' said the park keeper, poking Gruesome in the arm with his finger as he spoke, 'I'll drown it. All cats should be on leads.'

The very idea! A vampire's cat, or any other cat for that matter, on a lead. Gruesome hooted in derision. She hurried home with Bloodsocks, his tail lashing furiously, under her arm.

Gruesome was sad that she could no longer go in the parks. She loved the wide green lawns and bright

flower-beds. She also liked the swings, which she had tried out very early one morning when there was no one about. It gave her a lovely swoopy feeling inside which was nearly as good as flying.

Flying was something Gruesome never did now. She was well aware that people did not fly. She could tell she looked odd to the inhabitants of Trumpington, but she (more or less) fitted in. Flying anywhere, however, she knew would be unacceptable. People just didn't fly. They didn't seem to change their shapes, either, although she wasn't certain about this.

Another day Gruesome and Bloodsocks were in the 'Kwikbuy' supermarket in the centre of Trumpington. Bloodsocks was sitting quite cheerfully in the front compartment of the trolley. A little girl with a blue hair-ribbon saw Bloodsocks' tail sticking out of the trolley and pulled it – hard – and ran off.

'Sssssssssssssssss! Pssssssssss!' spat Bloodsocks, leaping out of the trolley. He knocked over sixteen packets of cornflakes, broke four jars of coffee and terrified an old lady, who hid behind the baked beans. The supermarket manager was very angry.

'If that animal sets one *whisker* in this shop again,' he said to Gruesome, 'I shall wring its neck.'

So Gruesome couldn't shop there any more. She was really quite sorry for she had loved wheeling the trolley up and down the aisles and peering at all the different sorts of food and drink.

Even crossing the road Bloodsocks was a nuisance. One day he sat down in the middle of the pelican crossing. While the lights changed from red to green, he methodically washed his ears and then started on his back. Long queues of traffic piled up on either side.

At last Gruesome managed to coax him on to the pavement but not before a taxi-driver swore loudly at her.

'Next time I see that cat,' he shouted, leaning out of the window and shaking his fist at her, 'I'll run over it. I'll make it into catburgers, so I will.'

Bloodsocks turned round and gave him a contemptuous stare.

After this, Gruesome was afraid to go anywhere with Bloodsocks. She tried to sneak out when he was asleep.

One day she came home from the shops (having left Bloodsocks dozing on top of the drainpipe) to find he had disappeared. Gruesome looked all over the back yard. Then she looked at the top of the drainpipe again to make sure. Then she looked all

round the back yard again. She even looked in the dustbin. He wasn't there.

She went inside and searched the house from top to bottom. She looked in the kitchen. Hairietta was on top of the cold tap busy eating her breakfast and didn't notice Gruesome at all. She looked in the front room. He wasn't there. She looked in the bathroom. Marcus (and friend) were jumping up and down in the wash basin trying to see into the mirror. They took no notice of Gruesome, either. There wasn't a trace of Bloodsocks anywhere.

Gruesome went out into the back yard again.

'Bloodsocks. Blood . . . socks,' she screamed piercingly. 'Puss, puss, puss, puss, PUSS.'

Windows opened up and down the backs. Someone threw a wellington boot over the wall. It just missed her. Two dogs started barking.

'Shut that noise,' someone shouted.

Gruesome went through to the front and looked out along Wellington Street. Surely Bloodsocks had not gone out on his own? Voices came into her mind:

'Next time I see that cat, I'll run over it. I'll make it into catburgers.'

'If ever I see that cat round here again, I'll drown it.'

'If that animal sets a *whisker* in this shop again, I shall wring its neck.'

The world seemed full of people who didn't like Bloodsocks, and now he had disappeared.

Whatever was she going to do? It was not as if she had any friends, either, Gruesome thought, apart from Big Pete the gravedigger. She chatted to people like old Mrs Thomas and the Patel twins, of course, but she didn't know them really well. Perhaps she should go to the Job Centre and see if she could get a job. Then she might make some friends. The thought of filling in more forms, though, put her off. Besides, she knew from all the people she saw at the dole office that there weren't any jobs to be had; and what job could she do anyway?

'What I have to do now,' thought Gruesome, 'is find Bloodsocks myself. It's no good thinking of the friends I haven't got.' Suddenly she jumped.

CRASH CRASH CRASH. It sounded as if someone were trying to knock the back door in.

8

A small boy with a bald head on which a smiling face had been painted stood there. He wore trainers, jeans, a T-shirt and a gold earring. He stared at Gruesome's long flowered dress and long black hair.

'What do you want?' asked Gruesome.

'Hiya. I'm Leotard Jones. I live up there.' He jerked a dirty thumb upwards. 'Can I come in? I've got something to tell you.'

'I'm Augusta, otherwise known as Gruesome Gussie,' said Gruesome as they moved into the front room.

'Hey, I like your picture,' said Leotard, going over to examine it more closely.

It was a collage from pieces of bone, mother-of-pearl buttons, dried leaves and twigs stuck on to a piece of black cloth and mounted on board. It showed a rattle of skeletons dancing in a graveyard. Gruesome had made it herself. Bloodsocks had helped by bringing her all the bones he could find from other people's dustbins.

'It's smart,' said Leotard. Then: 'Is this real?' he asked, pointing to one of the snakeskins.

'Yes,' said Gruesome, pleased with his attention. 'They're all vipers.'

Leotard sat down on a bright orange beanbag. 'Have you got a moggy?' he asked, as he pinched up the knees of his trousers.

'Bloodsocks!' cried Gruesome. 'Have you seen him?'

'Not exactly,' said Leotard. 'You see, I was looking out of our kitchen window. It looks on to the back yard, and I saw two men in the ginnel with a sack. The sack was wriggling about just like something was inside it. I thought I heard a funny noise as well – a sort of yowling.'

'You mean it was Bloodsocks? Someone's stolen him! But why? Where did they go? Where are they? Why didn't you tell me . . . ?'

'Keep your wig on,' said Leotard. 'I only just now heard you screeching after him. I didn't even know you had a moggy before.'

'What can I do?' asked Gruesome. 'Why did they take him? Who were they?'

'I know who they were,' Leotard said. 'Everyone knows them in Trumpington. It was Mucky Mike and Bruiser Bates. They're always up to something.'

'Would you like a drink?' asked Gruesome, suddenly remembering this was what people always asked visitors. Leotard nodded.

Gruesome brought in a tray with glasses of lemonade, a plate of biscuits and a jar of marmalade on it.

'They're dog biscuits,' Leotard said as he took one.

'Yes,' said Gruesome. 'I get them for Bloodsocks, really. They're good, aren't they? Try some marmalade on them.'

'They're *really* neat,' said Leotard, spreading marmalade lavishly on all sides.

They crunched away together for a few moments in silence.

44

'Why should they take him?' Gruesome asked at last. She was sitting cross-legged on the floor. (Chairs were something she could never take to, and beanbags were too squashy.)

Leotard curled his tongue round his mouth to lick off any residual marmalade. 'Perhaps they want money – they might send a ransom note. But you're not rich, are you? Not living here.'

'No,' said Gruesome. 'I'm unemployed. But if they kidnap a lot of pets, they could get quite a bit. I mean, everyone will give a few pounds, or whatever they can, to get their pets back, won't they?'

'Or they could want them for something else,' said Leotard.

'What?' asked Gruesome.

Leotard was silent for a moment.

'They might be taking them to sell to a laboratory for animal experiments,' he said at last.

9

Gruesome couldn't sleep a wink that night. She tossed and turned in her coffin and gnashed her fangs. She chewed one talon right down to the quick. She could never remember spending a single night before without Bloodsocks curled up on top of her.

In the morning she ate some chocolate biscuits spread with fish paste and drank a glass of potato juice. Then she sat down to wait for Leotard. He had to do his early morning paper round before coming to help her in the search.

Suddenly she heard the sound of her letter-box rattling and a letter dropping through. A car roared away, tyres screeching. Gruesome picked up the envelope. It was unstamped and not addressed to anyone. She ripped it open with a talon.

'wE HAve yOUr CAt iF YOu wANt IT bAcK aLIVe bRIng TweNTy POUndS IN oNE PouND noaTES miDnItE weNsDaY leAVE iT ON THe fLOOr oF THe foNE bOx ouTSiDe viCKRaGe laNE POsT OFFiCe puT tHe moNEy IN A brOWn pApeR baG iF YOu inFOrM thE pLEes yoUR CAt wILl Be kILLEd.'

The message was made up of printed letters cut out of newspapers and stuck on to a piece of card, capital and small letters all jumbled together. Gruesome was thankful yet again that she had learned to read.

47

'Twenty pounds. Not a lot,' said Leotard when he arrived later on. 'They must have taken some other pets as well. What are you going to do?'

'I'm going to pay the ransom, of course,' said Gruesome. 'I only hope they look after him well. He eats a lot.'

'Aren't you going to tell the police?' asked Leotard. 'They're pretty stupid – Bruiser and Mike. Though they must have someone helping them if they've got a car.'

'Of *course* not,' said Gruesome in alarm. 'You mustn't do that. I just want to get Bloodsocks back in one piece.'

'I wonder why they said tomorrow night,' said Leotard, scratching his head. 'Why not tonight? Probably so that you're really desperate by then.'

'Don't you know where they live?' asked Gruesome, striding up and down the room.

'No. They move about a lot so the police can't find them. I reckon they must have taken some more animals besides your cat, you know.'

'Where would they keep them?' asked Gruesome.

'Dunno,' said Leotard. 'Well, I'm off now. Nothing I can do except to see if I can pick up any news of them. See you! I'm going to have a little ferret around.'

Gruesome spent another miserable day.

She didn't go out.

No one called.

Whatever Leotard was doing, he didn't bother to come and tell her about it.

At last it was dark and she settled down in her coffin. First she opened her bedroom window wide –

it was so hot. Whatever the policeman said about not leaving your windows open at night when you were on the ground floor, she would die of heat-stroke if she didn't get some fresh air.

Gruesome woke up some time later with a start.

Someone (something?) had come through the window. She could make out a black shape against the wall lit up by the street-lamp outside the house. As Gruesome blinked herself rapidly awake, the shape metamorphosed in front of her.

'Hideous Hattie!'

'Augusta!'

– they screeched simultaneously.

Hideous Hattie, now in her more familiar vampire shape, collapsed on the floor in surprise and horror.

'Augusta! *You* living in a *house*. I never thought you would sink so low. Never!'

Her voice trembled with disappointment. 'I might have known. The first house I find with an open window – and what happens when I fly in, hoping for lots of lovely blood? I find *you*.'

'What are you doing in Trumpington, anyway?' asked Gruesome. 'This isn't your patch.'

Hideous Hattie shook her head woefully. 'Times are very hard, Augusta. Fresh blood is in short supply these nights. All this double glazing – it's nearly impossible to get into houses. No chimneys either – they've all got central heating; and if you do find an open window, you find you've flown into one of those wretched burglar alarms.' She spat on the floor. 'Poor Wuneye hasn't had a good meal for days.'

(Wuneye was Hideous Hattie's pet vulture. He

50

was a bird of unpleasant aspect with raggy, discoloured plumage and one bloodshot eye. No one, not even Hideous Hattie, knew what had become of his right eye.) As she said his name, Wuneye flew out from beneath her cape and perched gloomily on the wardrobe.

Gruesome looked at Hattie and then at herself. Is that what she looked like? Surely not.

Hattie looked at her as if reading her thoughts. 'Anyone can see this life doesn't suit you,' she said. 'Your face has gone quite pink. Disgusting, I call it. And where's Bloodsocks? And whatever have you got on?' Her voice rose incredulously as she gazed at the long pink nightdress Gruesome was wearing.

Gruesome had been so surprised to see a fellow-vampire again she had quite forgotten about Bloodsocks for a minute. Before she could say anything, Hideous Hattie turned to leave.

'I'll just have to look for sustenance elsewhere – I feel quite faint. Anyone live up there?' she asked.

'NO, Hattie.'

Gruesome sprang up. She thought of Leotard lying safely asleep in bed and waking to see Hattie's evilly-curved fangs poised over his throat.

'No you can't. You just try to suck blood from anyone in this street and see what happens. You're not to. I live here now. Leotard's my friend and so are the others.'

Hideous Hattie's eyes flashed green sparks. Her hair rippled with fury.

'Nonsense. Who's to stop me? Friends indeed. How can you be friends with *people*? We're all fading away through lack of blood.'

51

'What? Even Five-fanged Francis?' asked Gruesome disbelievingly.

'He's Four-fanged Francis now,' said Hideous Hattie, 'since his accident. But of course you don't know about that. I'm going now.'

'NO,' said Gruesome firmly. 'You're not going yet. Wait. I've got an idea which will help all of us.'

'Go on then,' said Hideous Hattie, who was just about to conceal Wuneye once more beneath her cape, 'but there had better be plenty of blood in it for all of us.'

'Yes,' said Gruesome. 'I think I can guarantee that, if you all help me.'

'Are you sure?' said Hideous Hattie, picking a grave-bug out of her hair and eating it. 'You know we can only go forty-eight hours without blood. Uncle Batticoop is looking quite peaky, and as for poor Annelid and Hirudinea . . .'

Gruesome shuddered.

'Listen carefully,' she said.

10

Wednesday didn't take as long to pass as Gruesome had feared. She woke up late because of her midnight visitor and had a brunch of kipper and honey sandwiches and a pot of thistle tea. Then she set about making up her brown-paper parcel. She tried not to think about Bloodsocks, whether he was hungry or thirsty or how they were treating him. Tomorrow he would be back with her, she told herself firmly.

Leotard didn't call all day. Gruesome was sorry. She thought, as she had told Hideous Hattie, that he was a friend, but he seemed to be keeping out of her way. She had even seen him in the Patels' and he had looked quite uneasy at seeing her. He'd dashed out without saying a word and the Patel twins, who were usually quite chatty, hadn't said much either. Gruesome watched television nearly all day, just looking at one programme after another without really seeing any of them.

At last it was ten minutes to midnight, and for once she didn't feel like getting into her coffin. She let herself cautiously out of the front door carrying a plastic bag with the brown-paper parcel inside. She was surprised to see so many brightly-lit windows in Wellington Street. Surely most people were in bed now?

Further down the street she caught up with old Mrs Thomas from across the road. She had her usual wide, almost flat, black shoes on, brown cloth coat and a paisley headscarf. Her brown plastic handbag was clutched firmly in her left hand. She looked round fearfully when she heard footsteps.

'It's a bit late for you to be out, isn't it?' Gruesome said. But Mrs Thomas's small dark eyes, set like currants in the watery suet pudding of her face, did not smile back.

'I reckon that's my own business,' she said. 'Good night.'

With that, she crossed over to the other side of the road. Gruesome was surprised. Old Mrs Thomas usually talked so much, it was hard to stop her once she got going. Whatever was the matter?

Then she realized that there was something else unusual about Mrs Thomas, quite apart from her unfriendly behaviour. What was it, she pondered, that was different about her?

Of course. She was *alone*. Usually Mrs Thomas was never seen anywhere, even at bingo, without Susie, her black Scottie. Whenever she scrubbed her doorstep, Susie was always to be seen sitting on the pavement nearby. She and Bloodsocks always got on well together. Now Gruesome knew where Mrs Thomas was going and why she was out late at night on her own. Susie, like Bloodsocks, had been kidnapped.

Gruesome looked round as she heard someone behind her. It was Mr Todd the butcher, a tall man with ginger hair and moustache (and *without* his Airedale terrier, Kenneth). On the other side of the

54

road she saw the Patel twins from the corner shop. Their rabbit must have been snatched, too.

Surely everyone was going to reach the phone box at the same time? Gruesome hurried as she heard the church clock strike twelve.

Before long she was on the Lower Barton Road. She looked round carefully before going into the phone box, and then laid her brown-paper package on the floor. She walked off, making a lot of noise, but dodged back when she got round the bend in the road. Then she climbed over the fence into a field and ran back until she was opposite the phone box. She positioned herself behind a tree. In a few minutes she saw old Mrs Thomas walking slowly towards the phone box. She emerged a few seconds later and started to walk back towards Trumpington. A minute or so later, Mr Todd the butcher sneaked into the box. After this the Patel twins appeared and the same thing happened again. Then there was silence.

It was dark except for the light from the phone box.

Gruesome waited.

A long time seemed to pass.

A few cars swept along the quiet country road between Lower Barton and Trumpington. Gruesome yawned and thought longingly of her nice wooden coffin.

SWOOSH!

A sudden wind stirred the leaves on the trees.

Then everything seemed to happen at once.

Pebbles crunched underfoot. A dark figure entered the phone box with a brief case and bent to pick up the brown-paper packages.

Five dark shapes flew menacingly overhead. As

soon as she saw them, Gruesome crept from her hiding-place.

The man came out of the phone box. As he did so, a panda car and a van drove up. Two policemen, carrying truncheons, dashed out of them.

The man dodged to avoid the policemen. At the same time, a crowd of girls and boys appeared. They leapt over fences and crawled out from under bushes and trees. The Patel twins and Leotard were there, and many others Gruesome didn't know. They were all shouting and waving umbrellas, rolling-pins, fish-slices and walking-sticks. They ran towards the man, knocking one policeman off balance while the other, bewildered by this unexpected mob, blew his whistle.

Mr Todd reappeared.

'What the heckers are that lot doing?' he shouted.

Bruiser Bates (for he it was) scrambled over a nearby fence and ran off across the fields, shedding brown-paper parcels as he ran.

'Stop him!' shouted Gruesome. 'He's getting away.'

The five bat-shapes, hearing her voice, descended as one vampire. Unluckily for them, at that very moment the other policeman sprang into life and lay about him with his truncheon, knocking down Uncle Batticoop, Four-fanged Francis and Hideous Hattie. They fell in a heap on the ground on top of two little girls in dungarees.

Annelid and Hirudinea, thoroughly upset, flew wildly about until they hurtled straight into the police van and knocked themselves out.

Gruesome, trying to rescue the two little girls, was hit on the head by a fish-slice.

By the time they'd all recovered their senses, Bruiser had made good his escape and was nowhere to be seen.

'You made a right mess of that,' said Mr Todd to the two policemen who, for lack of anyone to arrest, had taken the five recumbent vampires to the police van.

'It was this lot,' said the shorter policeman (PC Board) crossly. 'Kids! What on earth did you think you were doing? Ought to be in bed.'

He spoke to Leotard. The other children had dispersed rapidly to their homes when they saw that their plan to capture Bruiser as he came out of the phone box had failed. Leotard tried to explain.

'And what were that lot doing?' asked Mr Todd, pointing to the five vampires lying on the floor of the van.

Gruesome told him how she had planned to capture Bruiser with their help and frighten him into telling them where the animals were.

'And who told *you* about it all?' she asked the tall policeman with the very large feet (PC Gartside).

'*I* told them,' said Mr Todd. 'They took Kenneth – my Airedale. We had it all arranged.'

'What a mess,' said Gruesome. 'Three different plans. We all spoiled each other's.'

'Too right,' said PC Board, nursing a lump on his chin as he spoke. 'Should have left it to us.'

'But we've got to find where our pets are,' Gruesome said desperately. 'If Bruiser gets back to them before we find him, he'll kill them. We must find him.'

'That's right,' said Leotard. 'Or they'll try and get rid of them some other way. He dropped all the money, too, so he's got nothing to show for it. He'll be really mad.'

'And he knows the police are after him,' said Gruesome, scowling at Mr Todd.

Everyone was very cross and tired. They all started blaming each other. The policemen were as annoyed as everyone else because the sergeant would give them a terrible rollicking for messing up what should have been a simple job.

Gruesome was anxious to be on the move.

'We'll just have to catch up with Bruiser before he has time to do anything,' said PC Board. 'We can try all the places he normally hangs out.'

'What about this lot?' asked PC Gartside, pointing to the vampires. 'They don't look up to much.'

'All they need is some fresh blood,' said Gruesome. 'Then they'll be all right.'

'I'll take them home with me,' offered Mr Todd, who was secretly sorry he'd ever brought the police into it. 'I've got my car parked up yonder. I can easily spare them a steak or two from my shop. They can stay in my garden shed overnight.'

'Right,' said PC Board. 'That's one problem solved.'

While Mr Todd and PC Gartside carried the vampires from the police van to the car, Gruesome and Leotard picked up the brown-paper parcels.

'There are only three with real money in,' said Gruesome. 'Mine's one. I suppose old Mrs Thomas's is another. I wonder whose the third is.'

60

'Dunno,' said Leotard. 'It wasn't the Patels'. They cut up bits of paper.'

'Mrs Thomas was about the only one without a plan,' said Gruesome as she got into the police car with PC Board. Then to Leotard she added, 'Won't your parents be worried if they wake up and find you're not there?'

'No. I left them a note to say I was staying with our Bet. I do sometimes,' Leotard said, as he got into the van with PC Gartside.

'Come on, then,' said PC Gartside. 'We've not much time to find Bruiser.'

11

They had soon tried all the places Bruiser Bates and Mucky Mike had ever been known to live, as well as well-known haunts of theirs such as 'The Dirty Duck Inn' and 'The Pickled Trout'. No one seemed to know anything about either of them.

Gruesome was getting more and more worried.

'I guess we could try the animal lab next, Jeff,' PC Board radioed through to PC Gartside in the van. 'We might just catch them on the way there. If Bruiser's got back to them, they'll be trying to get rid of the animals and get some money for them.'

'Will there be anyone there at this time of night?' asked Gruesome, horror-struck at the thought of Bloodsocks being experimented on.

'There'll be someone, I dare say. Caretaker, perhaps.'

They headed down past the canal and turned into Bulteel Street.

'Look,' cried Gruesome. 'Down there.'

At the far end of the street, parked outside a terraced house, was a small yellow van. Two men could be seen hastily bundling things into the back of it.

As he stepped on the accelerator, PC Board radioed to PC Gartside. Bulteel Street was a very long street and there was no turning on either side until a good half-mile further on.

The men looked up as they heard the car. The van

doors slammed and it took off on two wheels, veering crazily across the road.

PC Board stopped abruptly, causing Gruesome to bump her head on the windscreen, as a man leaped out of the upper storey of a terraced house. It was the house where the van had been parked.

'Wait Bruiser, you sod. Wait,' he yelled. He landed on a bed of hardy perennials and before he had time to get up, PC Board had smartly handcuffed him and he was led off to the car.

'Quick, quick,' called Gruesome, leaping up and down on the front seat and gnashing her fangs in panic. 'They'll get away!'

'No,' said PC Board. 'Jeff's gone round the other way with the van. He'll head them off.'

They tore down the street, squealing to a halt in front of the first turning to the left as they saw the yellow furniture van (having met the police van) reversing at high speed back into Bulteel Street. It slewed to the left and crashed into a lamp-post, narrowly missing the panda car.

'Never was a good driver, that Bruiser,' said PC Board as PC Gartside and Leotard drove up, thus sandwiching the furniture van between them.

Bruiser Bates, a beefy-looking man with a small round head, his clothes covered with brambles and soil, jumped out.

'Come on then, Bruiser,' said PC Board. 'Your very own handcuffs. We keep them specially for you. Where's your mate?'

Bruiser nodded towards the van.

'Great, wasn't it?' said Leotard. 'I wish the chase had been a bit longer, though, don't you?'

'No,' said Gruesome. 'The animals might have been killed.'

PC Board opened the van doors. Inside, tied by string leads to hooks on the sides of the van, was Kenneth, Mr Todd's Airedale; and on the opposite side there was Susie, Mrs Thomas's Scottie. In a small cage sat a frightened and miserable rabbit. Two grey, mauve and white pigeons fluttered in another cage. And crouched on the floor was the dirtiest-looking man they had ever seen.

His face was unshaven and smeared with dust. His hair was long and matted. Trousers and T-shirt were stained with grease. Little bits of black fluff were visible between his toes. He smelled like a mixture of unwashed socks and overripe cheese. A fresh scratch down his left arm still oozed blood. He scarcely

noticed their arrival, he was so frightened. It was Mucky Mike. Standing a foot away, his back arched to a truly amazing height, claws extended, tail fluffed and wildly lashing, eyes green stars of fury, was a cat.

'Bloodsocks!' cried Gruesome. 'Bloodsocks.'

Never did a cat change so quickly.

At the sound of Gruesome's voice the hump relaxed, the claws retracted, the tail stopped lashing abruptly and re-formed into a question-mark.

Bloodsocks padded towards Gruesome.

While PCs Gartside and Board saw to Mucky Mike, who was almost relieved to see them, Bloodsocks circled slowly round Gruesome. He sniffed her dress and shoes delicately to make sure that it was indeed her. Then he leapt on to her shoulder, his eyes shading to a pale yellow as he began to purr like a dynamo.

The other pets, all looking dirty and hungry, were stowed carefully in the police van. Gruesome sat contentedly on the back seat of the police car with Bloodsocks on her lap, between Leotard and Bruiser.

'You'll have to stay with me,' she said to Leotard. 'You can't knock your sister up at this time of night.'

'Probably be morning, love, by the time you've both made your statements,' said PC Board.

12

Gruesome was so busy the next day she hardly had time to eat or drink. First she had to shampoo Bloodsocks thoroughly and apply flea-powder to his fur to get rid of the seemingly thousands of fleas he had picked up. Then she had to take him to the vet because he had caught a cold and his eyes were watery and bloodshot. Poor Bloodsocks was given an injection and prescribed a course of tablets. Gruesome pounded these up and hid them in his food. As well as all this, she had to prepare all the tastiest bits of food she could find to tempt him. In just a couple of days Bloodsocks had become quite thin and had lost his appetite. Furthermore, he wouldn't leave Gruesome for an instant (even if Gruesome had wished to leave him). Everywhere she went, Bloodsocks followed her.

Luckily, Leotard dropped in later (after he'd been home for a good sleep) to talk over what had happened. He promised to do all her shopping for her.

'Bloodsocks is very nervous at the moment,' Gruesome said, 'and I can't take him in the park or supermarket, anyway.'

'You must be really proud of him,' said Leotard, turning the gold ring in his right ear. 'He had that Mucky Mike nearly frit to death.'

Gruesome tickled Bloodsocks under the chin. 'I

bet the others were glad to get their pets back – Mr
Todd and the Patels and Mrs Thomas.'

'Yes,' said Leotard, 'and she was thrilled to get her
money back too.'

'But whose were the pigeons?' asked Gruesome.

'You know the people who moved in next to Mr
Todd's last week?'

Gruesome shook her head.

'The pigeons belonged to them. They're called
Musa.'

'Who was that man who jumped out of the window – the one they left behind?'

'He's called Len,' said Leotard. 'D'you know what they're calling him now down at the nick?'

'What?'

'Leftover Len,' laughed Leotard.

Gruesome gave him her shopping-list and some money.

'I'll be as quick as I can,' he said. 'You know, if I were you, I'd go to the dentist. You'd look much better without those fangs.'

'Never,' said Gruesome, in horror. 'What an idea. I'm a vampire, not a person, you know.'

'OK. Keep your wig on,' said Leotard. 'Your mates are staying in Mr Todd's back garden. He's written to the editor of the *Daily Pancake* about them. See you, Grue.'

Gruesome was very surprised the next day to find a photographer from the *Daily Pancake* on the doorstep. He wanted a picture of Bloodsocks. He looked askance at Gruesome and said he'd rather take a picture of Bloodsocks on his own.

Bloodsocks snarled and spat at the flash, and the delighted photographer quickly took a few more shots. Then he asked Gruesome a few questions.

'That's fine,' he said at last. 'Goodbye . . . er . . .'

'Augusta,' said Gruesome.

'Goodbye Augusta. Goodbye Bloodaxe.'

Bloodsocks turned his back on him.

A few days later two huge snaps of Bloodsocks, under the headline KIDNAP CAT, appeared on the front page of the *Daily Pancake*. One showed him looking fat and contented, the other a snarling ball of fury. (An inset captioned 'OAP's Heartache' showed a blurred picture of Mrs Thomas holding Susie and looking rather cross.)

'She was probably worrying about the dirty marks the photographer made on her doorstep,' Gruesome said.

Gruesome read the paragraph about herself with contempt.

'It's got nearly all the facts wrong,' she said to Leotard. 'They've called him Bloodaxe. And they've called me Miss Augusta Turner. Turner? Where did they get that from? *And* they've described me as a primary school teacher. Do I look like a teacher?'

Leotard looked without surprise at her. 'No,' he said. 'You look much better than any I've ever had. Anyway, my Mum says most of what they write in the papers is lies.'

The *Daily Pancake* took an interest in the kidnapping of the pets for several days. After its feature on all the pets who had been stolen, it turned its attention to the vampires who, after all, had attempted to catch Bruiser. It ran a special article about them which, although it expressed distaste for their general behaviour and bloodthirstiness, pointed out that, through their service to the community at large ('What service?' wondered Gruesome), they had tried to rise above the shortcomings of a deprived background. They had expressed their willingness to take on any outdoor employment (with a marked preference for nightwork).

The *Daily Pancake* issued a challenge to socially

aware companies to put their money where their mouths were and come to the aid of the deserving. The dearest wish of all the vampires was to return to their ancestral home in Transylvania, but in the meantime they were willing to 'get on their bikes' to find work.

Gruesome was not mentioned in any of this. However, she found she was famous on Bloodsocks' account. The very supermarket-manager who had forbidden Bloodsocks to set paw in his shop now welcomed them back wholeheartedly. He escorted Gruesome round his store and presented her with a voucher for a year's free supply of Pussiesteaks. The park-keeper presented her with a blue collar with a bell attached so that Bloodsocks could roam the park once more without harming the ducks.

Big Pete brought a wicker basket lined with a soft blanket and a big box of chocolates (all hard centres) for Gruesome. Lots of people, especially children, stopped to talk to them. Lots more waved to them from buses, cars, taxis and bicycles.

'You're famous, Bloodsocks,' said Gruesome.

Bloodsocks took it all as his due and accepted tins of best salmon, blue satin bows, clockwork mice and cod steamed in milk with aplomb.

13

Not long after this, Gruesome had more visitors. It was after midnight and the window was open again because it was, for once, a long hot summer. Through the window flitted five bat-shapes, quickly metamorphosing into Annelid, Hirudinea, Hideous Hattie, Four-fanged Francis and Uncle Batticoop.

'Augusta,' said Uncle Batticoop as they all draped themselves round Gruesome's coffin, 'we've come to talk to you.'

Bloodsocks mewed and flexed his claws on Gruesome's shoulder.

'All of us,' said Hideous Hattie.

Annelid, Hirudinea and Four-fanged Francis muttered in assent.

'Mm.'

'Yes.'

'That's right.'

Annelid flapped her bony hands about her face.

'So stuffy,' she said. 'How can you, Gruesome?'

Wuneye pushed himself out from under Hideous Hattie's cape, flew drearily round the room, and finally settled on the window-ledge. Bloodsocks padded over to have a word with him.

Four-fanged Francis sniffed loudly. 'Always thought you'd . . .'

'Ssh,' hissed the other vampires. 'Be quiet.'

Four-fanged Francis subsided grumpily.

'Tell me,' asked Gruesome curiously, 'how did you lose a fang?'

'You may well ask,' said Uncle Batticoop. 'You may well ask.'

Annelid, Hirudinea and Hideous Hattie clicked their fangs and hissed disapprovingly. Gruesome waited.

'Well?' she said at last.

'You may well ask,' Uncle Batticoop said yet again, 'but I'm not telling you.'

'Certainly not,' said Annelid.

'Absolutely not,' said Hirudinea.

'Too disgraceful,' said Hideous Hattie.

For once Four-fanged Francis had nothing to say. Gruesome almost felt sorry for him. Times had changed, she thought.

'However,' said Uncle Batticoop, 'that's not what we came for. Our friend, Mr Todd the butcher (a charming man), wrote to the editor of the *Daily Pancake* and he devoted a whole editorial to us in the paper.'

'In the paper,' said Annelid, Hirudinea, Hideous Hattie and Four-fanged Francis simultaneously.

Uncle Batticoop scowled. He went to the window and threw it even wider open. Then he opened the back door.

'How you can even *breathe* in here, I just don't know,' he said, flapping himself with his mould-encrusted black hat.

All the others fluttered their hands in agreement and Wuneye squawked.

'Your face, by the way,' he said, 'has gone the most unhealthy shade, and you've been *washing* your hair.' He looked at Gruesome as you might look at a slug in the middle of your ice-cream cornet.

The other vampires patted their dull and stringy tresses, infested with leaves, earth and graveyard bugs, complacently.

'Anyway,' Uncle Batticoop continued quickly, before anyone could interrupt him again, 'to continue. We have all been offered jobs. Night security guards for a big factory.'

'That's wonderful,' said Gruesome. 'Just what you wanted. Whereabouts?'

'In France,' said Uncle Batticoop. 'Dieppe. The manager was on holiday here and he read about our plight in the *Daily Pancake*. He wrote straightaway to the editor offering us the job – rather, jobs,' he corrected himself, catching sight of Four-fanged Francis's eagerly-opening jaws.

'But . . .' said Gruesome.

'We get a large juicy steak each per night as part of our pay,' continued Uncle Batticoop, 'so what could be better? He's paying our seafares over to France as well.'

'Wonderful,' said Gruesome, who was truly delighted to hear they would soon have the English Channel between them. That would put a stop to their midnight visits. She might get some sleep for a change. 'When are you going?'

'As soon as we've got our passports,' put in Hideous Hattie.

'In a few days, probably,' said Hirudinea.

'We've had our photos taken,' said Annelid.

'Without hats,' said Four-fanged Francis, looking sideways at Uncle Batticoop's crumpled topper.

'As I said,' said Uncle Batticoop, 'we're going by boat. It's much too far to fly.'

'We might fall into the sea and drown,' said Hideous Hattie.

Uncle Batticoop gnashed his fangs and stamped on his hat (which didn't make an awful lot of difference to it).

'Let me get to the point,' he said.

All the vampires stiffened and looked intently at Gruesome.

'There's room for you,' said Uncle Batticoop.

Gruesome was baffled. What did he mean?

'You mean room at Lower Barton churchyard?' she asked.

'No, no, no,' said Uncle Batticoop.

'No, no, no,' said Annelid, Hirudinea, Hideous Hattie and Four-fanged Francis.

Uncle Batticoop flashed reddish sparks. 'Room in *Dieppe*.' he said slowly. 'A job for you. Of *course* you want to go. They've provided a special camp site with a caravan near to the workplace. We don't have to sleep in it – it's just so we'll have an address. I asked about you, since the man seemed to think there were only five of us. We all know . . .' here Uncle Batticoop paused and looked round him while the other vampires nodded and hissed in agreement 'we all know,' he said, 'how debased and degraded you must feel at having to live here.' He looked round him with disgust, and spat.

'Debased and degraded,' said Annelid and Hirudinea, spitting in unison.

'Definitely demeaning,' spat Hideous Hattie.

Four-fanged Francis contented himself with an extra noisy spit.

'I know we cast you out,' said Uncle Batticoop. 'No doubt that is partly to blame for the unseemly and unsuitable life you now lead. Nevertheless, it has to be admitted that, had it not been for you, we should never have met Mr Todd and then we should not be going to Dieppe.'

'But . . .'

'No, you don't need to apologize, Augusta. We all forgive you.'

'As long as . . .' started Four-fanged Francis.

'You be quiet,' snapped Annelid, Hirudinea, Hideous Hattie and Uncle Batticoop.

'I do need to say something,' said Gruesome. 'I'm not coming. I'm staying here.'

'What?' chorused the vampires.

Wuneye left the window sill at the noise and circled round the room, beating his tattered wings.

'It's very kind of you,' said Gruesome, 'but I'm happy here. I like living in a house – well, I'm used to it, anyway. I've got lots of friends, too, and so has Bloodsocks.'

Bloodsocks mewed in agreement.

All the five vampires started talking at once. There was a great deal of howling, hissing, shrieking and spitting.

'*NONSENSE*,' said Uncle Batticoop, at last, by sheer noise quelling the other vampires. '*NONSENSE, PIFFLE* and *WONKYBONES*. Of course you're coming. You can't deceive us, Gruesome. We all know how you must hate it here.'

'But . . . ,' said Gruesome.

'But me no buts,' said Uncle Batticoop, 'as an old friend of mine once said. No need to thank us. We shall see you in a few days. Mr Todd is driving us all down to Newhaven.'

The vampires turned to leave.

'Once we have reached Dieppe, nothing about your stay in this . . . this . . . abode . . . shall ever pass our lips. That is a promise.'

'Never,' said Annelid, Hirudinea and Hideous Hattie.

'Yuk,' said Four-fanged Francis, taking a final disparaging look round.

Uncle Batticoop turned back towards Gruesome suddenly, knocking all the others into a jumble on the floor (with Four-fanged Francis underneath, Gruesome noted with satisfaction).

'At least one of us will come to see you before then and check you've got your passport and so on,' he said firmly.

Gruesome watched them leap backwards out of the window and fly off in bat-shape once more, down Wellington Street.

'It's funny,' she thought. 'I'm not afraid of them any more.'

Bloodsocks came over and rubbed against her leg. 'But we don't want to go to Dieppe, do we Bloodie?' she said. 'We're better on our own.'

She shut the back door and was about to climb wearily back into her coffin when the front doorbell rang.

'Stinking hellebore,' she muttered as she went to answer it. 'Oh for a nice quiet graveyard!'

14

It was the very last person she expected to see. Mrs Jones from upstairs was standing there, her hair in curlers, wearing a pink candlewick dressing-gown and pink mules with pompoms.

She looked relieved to see Gruesome.

Ever since she had read about her neighbour's cat in the *Daily Pancake*, she had basked in the reflected glory of actually living above her. It had given her a certain news-value among the workers at Trumpington railway station, and as a result she felt much kindlier towards Gruesome.

'Are you all right?' she asked, peering past her into the house.

'Yes of course,' said Gruesome. 'Come in,' she added regretfully. She hoped midnight visits on the part of her neighbours would not become a habit.

Mrs Jones stepped in and sat down on the battered old sofa in the front room. 'Boooooiiiinnnnggggggg,' it went as usual.

'I know it's a funny time to be calling,' she said, 'but I woke up and heard the most terrible noise going on. I tried to wake Dave but he was snoring away. I couldn't budge him. I heard these funny noises like a parrot or an owl as well, and then I saw your back door open . . .'

She was talking so fast Gruesome couldn't really understand most of it.

'So I fetched my old umbrella I keep under the sink for unblocking the drain – Dave'd go mad if I took any of his tools . . .'

Mrs Jones paused for breath and Gruesome offered her a dog biscuit. 'Thanks love,' she said and began to nibble at it without even looking at it.

'Then when I came downstairs with the umbrella, I saw your back door was shut again and it was deadly quiet. I was afraid you'd been mugged or something. So I thought I'd check up.'

What a nuisance those vampires are, thought Gruesome. Thank goodness they're going to Dieppe.

Mrs Jones started to apologize for disturbing Gruesome.

'No, it's all right. I did have some visitors,' Gruesome said. 'You've probably read about them in the paper. They're staying at Mr Todd's just now. I'm afraid they did make a lot of noise.'

'That's all right,' said Mrs Jones. 'I didn't know you'd been having a party.' She looked round the room vaguely. 'I like a good party,' she said, 'but there's always such a mess afterwards. Wouldn't have bothered you if I'd known.'

'I'm sorry we disturbed you,' said Gruesome. 'I should have told you about it, but it was rather unexpected.'

'Surprise party, eh?' laughed Mrs Jones, swallowing the rest of the dog biscuit. 'They're always the best. Well,' she stood up. 'I expect you'll be wanting to go to bed now. Clear up in the morning, eh?'

As Gruesome saw her to the door, she said, 'Was that a parrot I heard?'

'No, it was a vulture,' Gruesome replied. How to explain its presence? She racked her brains, and said at last, 'It came to wish Happy Birthday.'

Mrs Jones's face lit up. 'Really?' she said. 'Like one of them singing telegrams? My Bet had one for her Ron but she had a Gorillagram. Gave him a real surprise, that did. He nearly died laughing. I've never heard of a Vulturegram before. I'll have to get one for Dave's birthday. Mm. Yes. That's a right good idea.' She went off chirpily. 'Goodnight then . . .'

'Call me Gruesome. Goodnight, Jean.'

Over the next few nights Gruesome spent a lot of time in the privacy of her coffin worrying. She worried about the trip to Dieppe, about having to live with the other vampires again, about staying awake on the night shift, but most of all she worried about the raw steak they were each to be given. The more she thought about it all, the more she realized that she would much rather put up with the discomfort of living in a house than have to go back with them again. She shuddered at the thought of Four-fanged Francis holding her nose while Uncle Batticoop pushed the steak in her mouth.

Besides, she would miss her friends. Even Leotard's Mum had come down in the night to confront a mugger with an umbrella on her behalf.

'But how can I get out of it, Bloodie?' she said. 'They'll tell Mr Todd to come out and pick us up, and if I don't go, I know they'll come and drag me out of my coffin. You don't want to go either, Bloodie, do you?' she said, as she jabbed a fang into a tin of Pussiesteaks.

'Oooooowwwwwwww.   Aaaaaarrrrrrrrrrrrrrr!' she screamed, dropping the tin with a crash. Bloodsocks dashed over and rubbed himself round Gruesome's legs.

She had a terrible pain in her gum next to her left fang. She touched the fang gingerly. No, that wasn't where the pain was coming from. She poked about inside her mouth until she found the right one. It wobbled. She remembered Leotard's remark to her a few days ago. She would never have her fangs out but she didn't mind having one of her other teeth out. She pulled it.

'Aaaarrrrrr!' she screamed again. Bloodsocks jumped on to her lap and licked her face with his pink, sandpapery tongue. Gruesome rocked herself to and fro, supporting her head in her hands. At last the dreadful throbbing stopped.

'I'll have to go to a dentist, Bloodsocks,' she said. Bloodsocks mewed and then walked over to his foodplate and sniffed it.

'I can't open your tin,' Gruesome said. 'I daren't try the other fang. I'll cook you some fish fingers for now, and then we'll go out and look for a dentist.'

Bloodsocks sulked. He went to sit in the corner of the room with his back to Gruesome. He *hated* fish fingers. He didn't know what they tasted of, but it certainly wasn't fish.

Later, when Gruesome had got ready to find a dentist, Bloodsocks at first refused to go with her, but he relented when Gruesome promised him a treat for his tea.

They met Big Pete outside 'Trumpington Videos' and he directed Gruesome to a dentist's.

'Tell them it's an emergency,' he said. 'There are four of them. One of them's bound to take you on. You don't have to pay nothing if you're unemployed.'

Gruesome followed his directions and came to a red-brick Victorian house, with a short front garden sloping down to the road. A rhododendron bush extended lustrous purple blossoms to the sun.

A large sign saying DENTAL SURGEON hung above the front door . . .

Gruesome woke up. She had dozed off. She was lying in a . . . *bed*? Where was she? What had happened? She was wearing a long white dress she'd never seen before.

Her head felt muzzy. She looked round and saw that she was in a long room. There were a lot more beds.

A young woman in blue came over to her and explained to Gruesome that she was in hospital. She had fainted at the dentist's and they had sent for an ambulance.

Of course. Gruesome remembered now. The dentist, a young woman with red curly hair, had injected her upper gum. Gruesome hadn't minded that much. She hadn't minded the dentist extracting three teeth either. *That* hadn't hurt at all. But once they were out . . .

Gruesome shuddered as she remembered all the blood. The taste, the look, the smell of it made her ill.

'Toppling tombstones,' she cried. 'Bloodsocks! Where is he? He'll be starving.'

'Is that your cat?' asked the nurse. 'We found there was a cat in the ambulance yesterday . . .'

'*Yesterday*,' interrupted Gruesome. 'You mean I've been here all night?'

'That's right,' said the nurse, calmly. 'Of course, we can't allow cats in the hospital . . .'

'He'll be run over,' said Gruesome. 'He won't know where he is.'

'Don't worry,' said the nurse. 'One of the porters is keeping an eye on him and has found a shed outside for him to sleep in.'

When the nurse had gone, Gruesome went to find a phone. Leotard had given her his number when he had shown her how to dial. She rang him, told him of the visiting times and asked him to bring in a few things for her.

'OK. See you, Grue,' he said, and rang off.

Outside in the shed, on a shabby but comfortable cushion, Bloodsocks, dining on salmon and cream, was content. He always fell on his paws.

15

At last it was visiting time. Leotard arrived with lots of parcels and a large basket covered with a cloth.

'Here,' he said. 'Let's draw this screen round first – then everyone'll think you're on a bed-pan and they won't come noseying in.'

He took the cloth off the basket and out leapt Bloodsocks. He immediately snuggled down on Gruesome's stomach, purring vigorously.

'He's fine,' Leotard said. 'Bill the porter's been looking after him. Now, these grapes are from my Mum. She says you're a good sort even if . . .' He stopped and coughed. 'And Big Pete sent this.' He gave her a parcel, clumsily wrapped in a brown-paper bag and sellotape. 'He said you might not be able to eat much. And there's a card from old Mrs Thomas and one from the Patel twins. Oh, and Mr Todd's sent you this.' He put a large plastic bottle of Coca Cola on her bedside table.

Gruesome was delighted.

'Have a grape,' she said. 'I can only eat soft things just now.'

She unwrapped the parcel to find a six inch black plastic spider whose hairy legs quivered as she set it down on the bed.

'Neat, isn't it?' said Leotard.

'Don't, Bloodsocks,' said Gruesome. 'No, you can't eat it. Stop it.'

'I brought you a paper, too,' said Leotard. 'Look at this.'

WE FOUND THEM A JOB ran the *Daily Pancake*'s gleeful headline. It was, of course, a story about the vampires and the jobs they had been offered in Dieppe.

'They're going tomorrow morning,' said Leotard.

'What?' said Gruesome.

'That's right,' said Leotard, eating some more grapes and flicking the pips over the top of the screen. 'That's what Mr Todd says. You know on Monday I told you we were all going out?' Gruesome nodded.

'We couldn't go after all so we went last night instead. We went for a meal and then we went on to a pub. We sat outside under one of them stripey umbrellas. We were right late home because Mum got talking to some people we met in Benidorm last year. It must have been about half past twelve.'

'Ah!' said Gruesome.

'They were all there,' said Leotard. 'All five of them. We didn't see them till we got upstairs.'

Gruesome didn't need to ask who.

'Dad wanted Mum to tell them you weren't in. We didn't know you were here then. You should have heard her carry on. "That one down there's all right," she said, "but this lot. Just look at them. Bite your head off as soon as look at you, I shouldn't wonder. Look at that old grandpa in the hat – horrible he is – and that lanky one with his mouth open."'

'She meant Four-fanged Francis,' laughed Gruesome. 'He's so proud of his fangs, he hardly ever closes his mouth.'

'Must catch a lot of flies that way,' said Leotard. 'Anyway, they went round to the front to see if they could get in there. They were really cross, you could tell. In the end they flew off. Good riddance, my Mum says. Mr Todd's taking them to Newhaven tomorrow morning.'

'So I won't have to go after all,' said Gruesome. 'That's marvellous. I've been worrying about it for ages. Thank goodness they didn't know where I was. I can go home tomorrow, the doctor said. D'you know I missed a whole day? I went to the dentist Tuesday morning and when I woke up it was Wednesday.'

'Wish I could do that,' said Leotard, 'when it's time for school. I wouldn't mind missing the whole term.'

'It was worth having fang-ache for,' Gruesome said, 'not having to go to Dieppe with that lot. What time are they going tomorrow? I'll make sure I don't leave here too early.'

'They're leaving very early,' said Leotard pulling the spider out of Bloodsocks' mouth and waving it over his head. 'To catch the early boat. They think you've gone away.'

A loud bell rang.

'That's the visitors' bell,' said Leotard, eating the last grape. 'I have to go. Come on, Bloodsocks. Back in your basket.'

Leotard slipped the cloth over him just as the screen was whipped back and a cross-looking dark-haired nurse stood there.

'Why have . . . Arrrrkkkkkkk,' she screamed. 'Help! A tarantula!'

90

'Quick. You'd better go,' laughed Gruesome. 'See you back in Wellington Street tomorrow.'

By the time the nurse had returned with two more nurses, Gruesome was lying back quietly with the spider hidden under her pillow.

The other two nurses put their arms round the dark-haired one.

'Never mind, Tracey,' said one. 'It's the exams. You've been studying too hard. Come and have a cup of coffee.'

'But I could have sworn I saw a spider,' she said. 'It was huge, about as big as a saucer, with big hairy legs.'

'Ugh. Shut up,' said the other one. 'You'll have us all seeing it.'

16

The next day Gruesome and Bloodsocks went home on the bus to Trumpington. Bill the porter was very sorry to see Bloodsocks go, and gave him a packet of frozen kipper fillets as a parting treat.

'Real good company, he is,' he said. 'Bye love.'

Although she didn't arrive back at Wellington Street until eleven o'clock that morning, lo and behold, there parked outside her front door was Mr Todd's van.

Mr Todd was peering through Gruesome's front window as she came up.

'Hallo,' he said. 'I was setting out early, but they've cancelled the first sailing due to bad weather so we'll have to take the evening boat. Thought I'd just let you know, if you were here. Kicked up an awful fuss about you, they did. I had to tell them you'd be coming over later on. It's all right,' he said as Gruesome looked alarmed, 'they're asleep now.'

He opened the back doors of the van and Gruesome saw the five of them piled into the back, like a bundle of Guy Fawkes models waiting for a bonfire.

'I've got all their passports,' Mr Todd said, patting his jacket, 'and a phial of frozen blood each in case of need. I must say I'm glad they're off. My wife was starting to complain about them. They kept her awake at night.'

'Me too,' said Gruesome. 'But where's Wuneye, Hideous Hattie's vulture?'

'Is that its name? I never could take to that bird. It's in there somewhere. Mind you, I doubt if they'll get it through the Customs.'

'Goodbye Uncle Batticoop, Annelid, Hirudinea, Hideous Hattie and Four-fanged Francis,' said Gruesome. 'Bon voyage.'

They didn't acknowledge her presence by so much as the flicker of an eyelid.

Mr Todd slammed the back doors and locked them. 'I'll be off then.'

Gruesome waved till the van was out of sight.

No more midnight disturbances.

No more nips from Four-fanged Francis.

No more angry speeches from Uncle Batticoop.

She probably wouldn't ever see any of them again.

'Hiya,' said Leotard, appearing from the ginnel.

He'd washed the paint off his head now and started to grow his hair again. A very faint light stubble so far was all that could be seen.

'Felt like a change,' he said as he saw Gruesome looking at it. 'Anyhow, Dad kept nagging on about it.'

He followed her into the front room. She let Bloodsocks out of his basket. He immediately rolled over on to the floor and started to chew the head off the black plastic spider.

'I'll make a wokful of dandelion noodle soup,' said Gruesome. 'Want some?'

'You bet,' said Leotard.

Gruesome looked round at the dusty untidy room.

'It's good to be home,' she said.

Bloodsocks gave her a purr of agreement.